ROMANCE ON THE HIGH SEAS

LORENZO LAGO

Dedicated to all who love romance and adventure

Lorenzo Lago

CONTENTS

RIDE THE RICH LIFE OF SURFING

SIRENS, SOJOURNS, SPIRIT

ROMANCE ON THE HIGH SEAS

RIDE THE RICH LIFE OF SURFING

JUNGLE BUS

As we wind down through the mountains, toward the sea,
  I fill with youthful anticipation
I'm returning to a warm, tropical coast after time away

We twist and turn, circling our way through the jungle
  I notice the palm trees and bamboo are altered hues of this forever green

As the bus weaves its way, I catch glimpses of the coastline
  The sea's mystic white and sapphire blue explode in contrast to the jungle jade

Birds, radiant creatures of flight, strike color amid this ancient forest
  Perhaps, I'm also a creature of flight

I am the one American on this open-air bus
I'm surrounded by women and their children
  They are on their way to the marketplace
    There, the women will sell their fruits and veggies,
      flowers and seeds, shellfish and chickens

You name it, it's here
  and many of these exotic foods I can't name
I ask a woman what is this called...
  I repeat what she says, but her ancient dialect is difficult to grasp
I smile, she smiles, her kids smile

The men aboard the bus, they're off to labor in the forlorn jungle
  They carry machetes, a bit of lunch
    Each, with their traditional hat firmly in place

I wear my straw hat, light pants, tropic shirt
  I have to look the role
    No surf trunks here
One needs proper attire for this social encounter

My surfboard is in the back corner of the bus
My small backpack is by my side
Those onboard know I come for the waves that pound this section of coast,
 but they're not sure why I come so far

I don't need to explain
 This is my religion; this is what I do in my life

No need for philosophical banter
 No quotes from the great writers
  No words of wisdom from early surf pioneers

I come to fill my need, my craving
 I come to dance across the blue

Like Zorba, I dance till I drop
 Exhausted, my heart beats wildly
  My eyes look to the sea, toward the rolling ocean of life!

MOVING WITH WAVES

time passes in sweet sacred colors
    folding shades of rich blues and shadows

there is a feeling
    that takes over the soul
        when the sea reaches out for earth
            touches
                retreats
                    gathers strength
and again tosses its life upon the shore

no shyness
    no guilt
        but triumphs again and again

echo of a million years
    such ease
        grace
            surrender and sureness

sharing in strength and rhythm
    I keep, carry, and cherish

I am
    moving with waves

BAJA

The distant bay is bathed in intrigue
Symmetrical lines of swell wrap around the headland
Stacked one after another, the waves move with conviction

I launch upon the ocean,
paddle deep, and drop down the textured canvas
Pistons of blue unfold, one after another

Body, mind and spirit, such the celestial voyage

+++

Here, the sunrise appears so distinct
The night stars, they shine so intense!

The sky's rich timbre, the vast horizon,
the sandy stretches of the beach
Each, satiate my day

Every sojourn to this peninsula stirs my spirit

I never really leave this beach
It's always within my soul

THE FOUNTAIN OF YOUTH
(PONCE DE LEON, YOU WERE LOOKING FOR THE WRONG THING!)

We had to get out of the sun
only 10 AM, and shade is necessary

We've been surfing since daybreak
four hours of hoots and hollers
Remote surf has the allure that true adventurers seek

Decades of feasting on drama filled waves,
and these waves all drift together in my memory

I can still recall rides from years ago
The exact turn, the folding image of the wave's face
The power, and the joy!
The feeling of youth eternal!

Those that ride waves can relate
No one gave us an ad campaign to flaunt the thrill
We did not choose this lifestyle, it chose us

So, we ride as if it's our spiritual center
Our Mecca, our Fountain of Youth!

COCONUT RICE

overlooking a deep blue sea, the palapa sits peacefully
a gentle cove, rests below
the view here is vast, and beautiful
dawn and sunsets are always distinctive

deep water envelops the locale, so to get to the best waves for surfing,
we make a swift passage through a jungle

the path, thick with mosquitos
so, it's essential to wear a long sleeve shirt, and trousers
for any exposed skin, is attacked by a plethora of these vexing pests

this is the daily routine till we get to the estero
to get to its opposing shore, we employ a dugout canoe to span the salt-water river
a swim or a paddle across the expanse would be refreshing,
but there are stories of crocodiles that silently slither below the surface

we reach a pure white beach, spotted with seashells
the surf break sits directly in front of the river mouth
strong south swells hit this break with secret intensity

the wave breaks at a double peak, that shifts ever so slightly
we paddle our surfboards into one peak, and then drive through the second peak
this makes for a nice ride through the inside section
on big days, the double peak comes together as one farther out to sea

these are the days that I remember the most
thrilling rides and heavy paddles
the surfing lasts for hours

we regroup on the sand
reflect on the waves, and rest
we then cross the river, and again, through the land of bloodsuckers

back in the palapa we make eating a priority
we have been sustained on fish, but our staple is rice
our gourmet meal is usually coconut rice
rice with coco milk, coco meat and honey
our sweet tooth satisfied

these days, my travels take on an altered appearance
my escapades differ from my earlier days of coconut rice
they may not be as bold, daring or rugged
but the scenery, the inspiration, the sensation is just as grand
surfing bold frontiers still stirs the inner juices
yes, the spirit of adventure, and living the life, rings true!

OLD FRIEND

Old friend, it is good to see you again
  it's good to share some waves
You have always worn your heart on your sleeve
  I honor that in you

Sharing waves with an ocean comrade can make for a great day
  Our ocean passion and the sea's healing energy is just plain fun!

I've had this sincere bond with friends from Hawaii to Oaxaca
  And from cold water to the tropics
Heroic adventures all…
  These times always ring true in my memory

My amigo, I have a grand mental photo as you style across a wave
  Your smiling face expresses the story so well!

And my lucky day, here comes another thriller
  I turn, and stroke into the blue canvas,
    carve, and then soar into a massive tube…yahooooo!

Totally stoked, we both hoot and holler in elation!
  This is the life to live!

THE JUNGLE

ocean
a narrow stretch of sand
and the jungle

a jungle that is thick and electric
it pleads and begs creatures
humans included
to look deep into its heart

the endless shades of green coax us to think
we could live within its vines
sometimes, the only safety from the sun

but I do not trust those fences of flora
or the insects, reptiles, mammals
that wander through its night

the jungle always seems hungry
I fell into an adventurous lifestyle
but that doesn't mean I dare to sneer at nature I don't quite understand

years ago, I had this same feeling on a sailboat out in the middle of the ocean
I just couldn't get my body and spirit
to take the constant battle with the sea
it is very simple
sometimes our priorities have clarity
'get off this ocean'
'don't go in this jungle'

yes, priorities and clarity
like finding one's soul mate
the truth of falling in love
like parenthood
raising a family
we rejoice in how clear it all becomes

now, I will ride these waves
later, and with plenty of daylight
I will walk this narrow stretch of sand to the village
I'll talk of surf, colors of the day
but I'll leave my insecurity for my journal

WAVES OF BRAVADO
An Adventure with Paul Georghiou
Brother my Soul Bows to Yours!

From an altitude of three thousand feet, we scan the island below. I share this space with my friend, Paul, the owner and pilot of this Comanche 250 aircraft.

Summer is best time of year to surf the waves that tap the island's coast. It's the afternoon's prevailing onshore wind that blows across the island's west coast that develops into an offshore breeze on the island's east side. And, if a solid southern hemisphere swell is ensuing, it is the addition of that prevailing offshore wind that will make for inspiring surfing conditions!

But we've made this sojourn in winter, and no south swell is breaching the island's eastside. Auspiciously, as we soar above, we do notice waves breaking on island's southwest coast, and these waves look like they can be ridden.

After landing the plane, and with the assistance of a fisherman, we obtain passage around the island. We stow our surfboards and gear aboard his boat, and hold on for a bumpy ride to the east side of the isle.

Anchored within the calm of a bay, Paul and I launch from the boat, and paddle toward the upper point of the bay. We are both smiling in anticipation! Though, as we near the breaking waves, we observe that the height of each wave is greater than we expected! Yes, there's far more power than we anticipated. Waves are exploding on the reef in epic proportions! **IT'S GIANT!**

I take a few deep breaths. Inhaling and exhaling, in and out, and focus on gathering the bravado vital to ride these massive waves.

After centering myself, I smile and laugh. And this laugh seems to set me free of any apprehension. I decide to look fear in the face and journey on!

In truth, fear has no place in big surf. Or in life for that matter. Caution, yes! Fear, no! Yes, just laugh it off and go for a surf! Just smile, Lorenzo, it'll be fun!

We continue to paddle towards the oncoming waves. A large set approaches from the horizon, and we are now in position to catch and ride these beasts.

I focus on the takeoff and driving down the wave's face. So I go, and I ride. Paul goes, and he rides. The surfing is heavy, scary, spectacular and fun! Such an epic surf session!

We each get our share of big, thrilling waves! And, we both get our share of being pinched a few times by some outside sets, but the surf session is all glory!

Late that afternoon, we admit to some hesitation about paddling into a few monsters! And, with glasses held high, we toast the waves and the rides we scored!

It's amusing how letting go of fear can be so liberating…in waves, and in life!

MANY YEARS AGO

Peaceful Maui morning
I walk the western shore

I carry swim fins, mask and snorkel, and Hawaiian sling
No real swell, so free-diving for fun

+++

I drift the shallows of a sacred bay
Coral and sea creatures are plentiful

+++

I spear a beauty

A friend affirms, that centuries ago this fish was only taken for royalty
A prize that has already joined others within my pack

So, we honor the Kahunas, and prepare the day's catch over an open fire
Like the ancient Hawaiians, we eat, laugh, and chant song

+++

I am just a visitor here
No native blood runs through my veins
But I come as friend, and with an open heart

The swaying palm welcomes me
Exotic orchids and fragrant plumeria entertain me
The trade wind whispers aloha

And I embrace all of you as my friend

TRADES

trades

blowin

tips of waves

back over

rainbows

around

SAILING HOME

This ocean I'm sailing, is so vast
What am I doing here?
This was my dream, but I am not sure this is my destiny?

This isn't like me
Mr. Easygoing, is not so easygoing
I'm a small speck on such a large liquid surface
I mean, such an expanse of blue water!

I am daydreaming about land
perhaps a small beach on a palm-lined cove

I'm bodysurfing in warm, clear water
The woman in my life is sliding alongside of me

Every so often, my feet touch the earth below the surface
There is a smile on my face
I understand this role of my life
I have lived it for decades
This is where Zo Lago belongs!

Time to anchor the boat, and remain on this palm-lined cove for as long as I
can!

PHOTO, A THOUSAND MILES AWAY

I carry your photo with me
kept within my journal of poetry in progress

I can be on the other side of the world
riding waves on a lost island
resting in the shade
a cool drink in hand
and there is that look on your face

I took this photo after we made love

I would like to boast
I'd like to share the photo with others
but I don't
I respect how free you are with me
how you thrill in the wild war of making love
how you rejoice in what we share

I see it on your face in this photo
you've got the power
you know I'm thinking about you and your body
all wrapped around me
right now
on the other side of the world
a thousand miles away

TROPIC STORM

it's midnight
I've just arrived on the point
a raging storm fills this tropic night
I am not sure if I have ever walked in such blackness

torrential rain is soaking the ground and me
thunder shatters the world like a battle between the gods up on Mount Olympus
the screaming winds possess a haunting whistle

I'm attempting to navigate to a friend's home further up the point
it is foolish to be out in such weather
but arriving so late, I've nowhere to go but my determined destination

ever so often, great lightning manifests in this darkest of nights
in an instant
one split second
everything below the banana trees is like daylight
bright with the strength of a thousand flashbulbs bursting
it is surreal

for that one second, I see I'm going in the right direction
what would take me five minutes on a balmy afternoon
is lasting an hour tonight

finally I arrive at the home of my friend
a brick building, with a good roof
and secure window screens

"hey bro, it's Lorenzo, you awake?"
some slumber detained, my amigo greets me
with a hand shake, a warm hug, and few slaps on the back

we talk over candlelight for an hour, take a toke
we discuss waves and big days on the point
and how tomorrow's surf may shape up
exhausted, I fall into a soft cot on the porch
I sleep deeply

the storm passes in the early morning hours
and at daylight, a steady offshore wind washes down from the mountains
through the deep lush valleys
and this wind eventually touches the waves that are filling in the point

this offshore wind feathers the top of each wave's face backwards
and holds the breaking wave's energy from exploding for a few seconds longer
a bit of magic

perfect conditions for surfing
seeing and living this miracle is what real surfing is all about
waves break all over the planet
and in so many scenarios
but right now, this is like slipping into the Garden of Eden

this is my fifth time here on this coast
I've made this journey by car, plane, train and sailboat
each pilgrimage, a very eventful sojourn
filled with mechanical mishaps
cultural awakenings
new friends
sunrises
banditos
wild weather
wild women
lots of laughter and some fear
luckily, I have survived these passages into manhood

this morning, Neptune has opened the floodgates
the waves are marching into the point
long, plentiful walls of water are filling in from First Point through Third
there is a direct takeoff spot, but one can pick the wave up all along the point
a grand, strong wall of water with an easy takeoff
the richness and luxury of sweeping, regal bottom turns
the smooth, forceful drive towards each folding section
and inside cathedrals of tubes
if only I could bottle this surf so I could take a swig whenever I wanted

we have a great time for hours
we only share the surf with a handful of others

as the day moves on, I consume ample food
I nap for an hour
early afternoon brings heavy humidity to the air
the wind is still
there is a silence to the birds
there is a separate scent that accompanies this sky
you can feel the direction of the energy
this is how a tropic day moves in the rainy season

there is no question that it will rain soon
there is an eminent storm brewing
it'll start with a serene, gentle touch
and then it will soon move into a strong downpour
life at the point
a tropic storm

OCEANA, SONG OF THE SURF

blue lady with your rolling thunder
   getting to know you better
      getting to know what makes you move

love to touch your silky skin
   love to lose myself in your glory

with your sacred expression
   you are free
      and you make me free

blue lady
   I am gliding
      on your silver gown

bathed in your sweetness
   captured by your charm
      I am free

ISLAND DANCE

island calls to me
    away
        I am free

island whisper
sunny sands
    time drifts with the tide

sky of soulful wanderings
wind sails my soul
    toward
        an endless horizon

island calls to me
    your voice of truth
        given way to newborn youth

silent traveler
got a nice day
    under my feet
goin to just float
    with this warm wind

REEF HOUSE

drifting swells
press this island
my bungalow
facing the long waves

this reef
fills with waters of life
bathed in a warm summer dream

the beach life
gives me all I need
a sense of strength
a simple intoxication

riding waves here
like heaven
new each day
sky
ocean
clearness in the glow of sunrise
and in my mind
dreams with voice

fruitful ocean
bathing in your playground
new world adventure
my heart beats in time with the pounding waves

my friends, you can share this peace with me
small blessings when you visit

and woman of my life
you fill this shack
with your beauty
your scent
your spirit

you make this sky and ocean come alive
with the touch
that only another soul can enlighten

ROMANCE ON THE HIGH SEAS

.

SIRENS, SOJOURNS, SPIRIT

GOLDEN ARROW

Myth has it that Cupid's mother was Venus, the Goddess of Love
Cupid's father was Mars, the God of War

So, Cupid is cunning, and he is a troublemaker
he has the duality of love and war
Cupid shoots golden arrows so one will fall in love,
and lead arrows so one will fall out of love

+ ⊢+

In the past, I have been to battle
I armed myself with the defenses of flowers and emotions
and still, arrows of gold, and lead, slipped within my spirit

My Empress, one of Cupid's flaming golden arrows has pierced my skin
This arrow has driven deep into my heart, and deeper into my soul

This is a profound wound
I'm bleeding emotions that I've never felt
I'm oozing with love's infectious symptoms
My fever is great, and I don't want it to stop

Your beauty overwhelms me
My infatuation is insatiable
I am delirious with visions of you

My Sweet Angel, you prowl within the forest of my world
And from the darkest night ever, you travel on the river of your soul
I'm not lost in this darkness, but set free

WOMAN

this moment of intrigue
    this spell of love
these innocent and gallant emotions
you and I both held captive
    both set free

in a simple instant we aroused an appetite for romance
    emotions awoke from slumber
    a new frontier expanded in colors

the sphere of our love
    reason enough
    not to discover the boundary

sweet enchanter
    you have made me
    wanted and needed
    bold and strong
    alive

the smile on your face
    ignites a flame that heats my heart
    this torch of love melts my soul

I've come along for this ride
I abandon memories of past lovers
women with their soothing, eternal scent
    replaced and rewarded
    with a new woman's fragrance
    your fragrance

I can not seem to get enough
your smile says it's not enough
    so take Lorenzo
    and I take
    I want
    I feast

I won't be satisfied with a moment
I need a season of you
I want your bouquet
    to fill my house
    to fill my time
    to fill my life

THE SEARCH

long lost lover
keeper of my heart
    the search for your
        complete surrounding warmth

finding the path
    soft voice of your music
        gentle on my face

clear water truth
    bathed in your sweetness
I move upon distant seas
    the treasure
        is your closeness
    touching
      moving
        within my soul

HER KISS

Consider the first moment of our embrace
Lips touching that never touched before
You felt warm, perfect

I know this kiss
like oxygen to a dying man
gasping for air
his breath restored
His mind and spirit saturated with some potent intoxicant
This is the promise that everyone wants on their lips

I've felt it before, with other lovers
It seems so long a time since I have tasted such a femme feast

This is magic, tender, erotic
Like a majestic melody that's been going on in my head
awoken, and to be sung

Press your lips to mine, and again
take me away
take me

JOURNEY'S END

From the loneliness, I charted my voyage
Setting a course toward the island of your soul

My sails filled with the warm winds of passion

Anchored now, I claim this land for myself
I explore your scented paradise, and taste the fruit of the rousing femme

For years, I survived storms
fought pirates and souls
smuggled dreams and bodies

And, at last, I arrive at the shores of your soul

Color my journey lover, embrace me
burning lips, burn my lips
burning skin, burn my skin

Have I always dreamed you?
Loved you, naked and native

Shall my voyaging cease?

The summer of your soul is so inviting!

FINALLY, HERE IN BED!

early evening
I'm staring at your lips
beauties
spectacular, yes!
and meant to be kissed!

the intoxicating scent of your body
igniting my imagination
romance and animal
rapture

dancing
touching
our arms
around
we are moving
    into this loving
wonderfully
no stopping us now!

this lagoon of your youthful, eternal splendor
this shimmering expanse of your beauty
the lure and woo of an angel
and my thirst for a new landscape

this thrill of a new wind
    glorious and persuading
        convincing
easily, my heart opens to heaven on earth

sweetest of sweet candy, you are playing with me
I have to laugh at myself as I lose myself

I soar across the water of your presence

dancing
touching
our arms
around
we are moving
    into this loving
wonderfully
no stopping us now!

DEVOURED

That beach walk
the one where we made love
great love
far away from everyone
off in the sun
we couldn't take it anymore
we had to devour, and be devoured

The simple truth of new romance
just creatures of the earth
discovering pleasure
undressing
dressing
undressing

Spirit Friend, how did we miss each other for so many years?
Was it the charm of all women that kept me from seeking my true ally?

My love, let's celebrate this embrace
Let us spin within this passion, and soar!

GOSH

Oh!
you stood up, and the sand clings to your body
and your thigh is a sculpture in grains of sand
Michelangelo couldn't have made anything more beautiful
or more complete

the sand is not falling off as you walk toward the ocean
I am grinning
I find you so beautiful

you are art,the spirited femme
you are the soul of a million women

you are the sun grasping the planets
you are the meaning of heaven on earth
and from the center of earth, you are gravity
keeping this world in flow and rhythm

Ah!
look at the way that sand clings to you!

ROCK AND ROLL TONIGHT

the suspense of your arrival
moments
    till you are deep within my arms
moments
    till we both surrender

the grand anticipation of seeing you
    come through the door
your body dancing as you walk inside my space

naked, you are radiant
like nothing I have ever seen
your whispers sing sinfully
your scent so sweet
like the scent of plumeria,
    gardenia
or a dark red rose
    a red that is almost black

my Venus
tonight, we will awaken, soothe and share our senses
tonight, we will caress, compliment and celebrate
tonight, we ignite the spirit with dazzling romance

SCHOLARS

for centuries
scholars
have attempted
to define heaven

I am tasting
the nectar
of your flower
you are gently
touching your breasts

your eyes are closed
you are moaning
and as you abandon all control
your head lifts up and back

your orgasm

this is heaven

ISLAND MAGIC

this is a French island
each day fragrant flowers decorate the tables and bar
we wear some of these small flowers behind our ears
we are dining on lush local fruit and fresh tuna
we are drinking fine, rich wine
and strong espresso

local young women sit in shallow water
their small bathing suits fit comfortably on the sandy bottom
with bare breasts
dark brown skin
long black hair
they inspire artists to make them unforgettable
and who could forget them

this a grand time of our relationship
we are in the habit of kissing at least two dozen times every hour
people near us think we are newlyweds

I can not get enough of you
and thankfully
you can't seem to get enough

so we lock ourselves away from everyone
for long periods of time
we still get plenty of sun
we bathe in the blue lagoon
but we can not help ourselves
we are intimate and excessive

I like the way you are in this heat
what has gotten into you
in this sensual sauna you lose all and any apprehension
you seem to be living out your fantasies here
the woman within you has become a seductive animal
you make love to me, sleep, make love, sleep
and love again

sweetheart, are you trying to wear me out
this is the way I like it
please keep trying

TIME IN FRANCE

you didn't feel well
you had a sad face
you told me to have a good time
so I'm exploring on my own

this Mediterranean life fits me quite well
since my first visit long ago
I've always felt comfortable here
I feel as if I belong within this French ambiance

I wander down stylish tree lined avenues
past 18th century mansions
I marvel at carved historical fountains
centuries of stories and tales mixed within the marble
as I enter the old section of town
I scan the azure water of the sea
the water is ever present in this setting
the sun glistens across the sea with ageless emotion

I stop at a reassuring café for a drink
it sits in an ancient square
an enduring 16th century church towers up the street
old cobblestones connect the café with other well groomed shops
these gathered establishments have a small fertile park
it rests in the center of the square

I am soaking in the atmosphere
this is so different than home
I like this lifestyle
I love the flavor of this town
the rolling hillsides that echo down upon the village
the amazing cuisine that fills the town's tables
and the wine
the wine that is always rich

I like the French people
they talk as if they know the pastry
the coffee
the vineyards
the dinner one is planning with empowered awareness

the day moves from morning to afternoon
I walk through quaint poetic streets

this end of town has a modern touch
but you can tell its roots are old
from Napoleon to fashion models
from fishing boats to racecars
from sacred recipes to engaging chefs
this is tender
this is fun
France, I could live here

I must make tonight very special for you
because you are so very special to me

I will shop for tonight's dinner ingredients…

first
to stop at the wine shop
a bottle of your best please
the owner always makes the correct choice for me

next, the aroma of the cheese shop has me tasting and buying
on to the open air market
to choose some lean meat
the woman at the counter talks only of freshness and quality
teasing my senses
I squeeze into a pastry shop for some absolute works of art
I stroll into a floral wonderland for a fragrant gathering of blossoms

I have what I need to entertain you this evening
you need to be cheered up
we need to fill our night with a romantic pastel of mood and color

you are my French beauty
your hair lies just so
my thirst for that sweet sexy look on your face
your body always moves with style
my ravenous hunger for you naked
from the aroma of your skin
through those long legs
you bring out the best in me
man and beast!

what a thing of beauty
what a woman
you are correct and decorated
all women should be as exquisite as you

your look
your taste
you kiss as all women should kiss
you are so potent
I keep coming back for more

you adorn me with your love
I want this evening together
to bring out the best
in you, and in me

I walk through the door, into our warm kitchen
there is wicked smile that lights your face
what a kingdom you have painted across your life
France, I could live here

YOUR DEFINING NECK

I could write lines of alluring verse about your lovely face
It would be easy to accommodate the pages with entertaining pleasure
All the eloquent ways you flaunt your beauty
Embellished stanzas to illuminate how well you persuade

But I want to focus on your neck,
And the way it dares to be kissed, the way it initiates caresses
Your lustful neck, and the feeling I get when my lips applaud its skin

When I stand near you, I just as soon lift your head this way and that
so to get at all the daring angles of your convincing influence

My exploration has to be thorough
I have to be sure my kiss settles just where you desire
This pleases you, and a smile appears on your lips

At twilight, your neck settles elegantly like poetry
At daybreak, it rests gracefully like a Rodin sculpture

Defining, and so irresistible

HERE YOU ARE

here you are
seeing you again
has it been years

I have not thought of you
for such a long time
and
here you are
standing
just inches from my mouth

you were always beautiful
but now, many moons past
you look even better

that was a fun time
so long ago
we just needed each other
as friends
as lovers

we never took it too far
we laughed
we kept our bodies touching
we said goodbye

and here you are again

you are very tempting
you may have another lover
I should not pursue you
if I can only persuade my animal to just smell the air
linger and move on

I should just take you in my arms
suggest that we should be very close again
as close as your blouse is clinging to your body
as close as my glowing imagination sings

can I put my arms around you
circle you in warmth
gather your hair and waist within my world

as you kiss my cheek
smile through your farewell
you tell me
how nice it is to see me again
how funny it is that I am standing in front of you
just inches away

you had not thought of me
for such a long time
you sigh how we were meant to meet again
that we should get together
that was a fun time
so long ago

as you walk away
you look over your shoulder
and with a tender glance
your eyes seem to whisper back
call me…

SUNGLASSES

I've seen you on this beach before
we said our small hellos
today
we are talking here in the summer sun
we have met
introductions have taken place

you're hiding behind your sunglasses

there is a drop of water
on the corner of your mouth
from that last cool drink

should I slowly move my lips across your lips
taste that drop of water
I want to feel your breath
I want to breathe you
I want

can you tell that's what is on my mind
or
is there a lover waiting at home for your return
patiently waiting
ready to embrace you
kiss you
or
are you glad we are talking
glad we met
glad to be looking at me
from behind those sunglasses

WE CELEBRATE MY FAVORITE TIME

there is romance
when we never want it to end
nights of love don't stop in the morning
daybreak just puts more light and beauty on your body

we kiss as morning warmth
slices the cool air away
we find ourselves within the lure of soothing passion

together we know this is perfect

I can hear your whispers
and calling for more
I can smell the love of your body
I admire your absolute pose
we are so close
we are breathing in each other's soul

your time has arrived
you can not stop what is coming next
this moment of ecstasy
this is my favorite time
you are every part of this space
you lose yourself and you find yourself
you are complete
you are every woman
right now, giving and taking
you are pure
correct
savage
all that is graceful on earth

I AM LOOKING FOR PARADISE

a new woman has become part of my daily desire
the harmony of each note we play together
resonates as a melodic chord

our innocent introduction
the sharing of our dreams
understanding our connection
our first opportunity to kiss and caress

is this paradise

I feel nurtured
open to this path that greets me
I cherish the moment
I savor the hour

and you are gracious
grand
sexy
you let your heart and body
give to this bliss

is this heaven

passion play
you are a wise and joyful lover
I thrive in this jungle
of electric heat
I flourish in this gypsy garden
the habit of you
the narcotic of you
like a mysterious passage

I move into paradise

GALATEA

blessing of Venus

    marble to flesh

        myth to emotion

            the embrace of the first kiss

blessing of all Venus women

    marble awakes to caress flesh

        forgetting and forgiving the myths

            brilliant emotions become alive

                the embrace of the first kiss

THE BATH

we meet by an illuminating glow of candlelight most every night
our special rendezvous surrounds us in hot, healing water
we float in bliss
our time to caress and carry on
talk and touch
lather and laughs
it all becomes a passion play
we shampoo each other's hair
that feels so good!

we kiss
clean kisses
wet kisses
brilliant kisses
sweet spice of lust
we dry each other with soft towels
we are squeaky clean!
our evening is just beginning!

my siren, my treasure
standing by our bed
you are almost a dream
with your hair pulled back
skin shining
showing off your female instincts
nice and naughty
you are hypnotizing

you know what you do to me
divine creature
you flirt with me
and I make an attentive audience

let us seize the moment
play and persuade
tickle and tease
coax me
seduce me
squeeze me
hold on sweet and don't let go
let's get scorched silly by this exchange

WEDDING DAY

a sweet Sierra sunrise rests on the profile of your face
I admire the soft lines of your silhouette
I wonder if Raphael or De Vinci
had a model with such stark beauty

today a light, early morning mist covers the ground of these sacred mountains
I attempt to write some verse about how I am always awed
by this communion of sky and land, and our connection to it

yesterday you said this is our cathedral
without walls or an alter
without hymns and prayers
only nature's service of wisdom was heard here

it's preached by the hawks, jays and owls
echoed through the trees when the afternoon breeze blows
it is perceived in the stream that we bathe in each day

we baptize ourselves in this fresh spring that dances through the hills
reborn in this spiritual healing water
water of melted snow from the highlands
so this baptizing is so very cold!
invigorated and cleansed we laugh
you say I am handsome, I say you're more beautiful than ever

the last few days we have not spoke in excess
we listen intensely to what nature is whispering

you've been shooting lots of photos
all have strong feeling and awareness
you're quite an artist
each tree you focus on is noble and distinguished
each peak stirring and dramatic
you're capturing these images
you are keeping it all as pure as it sits

loving you is always a majestic experience
but here in this setting
we both feel there is special meaning
something different is happening
there's a festival going on of exploding senses
each caress is more tender then the last
our sharing has become a ceremony

we do not scem to care that we are in so deep
that this must be the next step in our relationship
something new is in the air
it feels correct and sensational
here today in these mountains
but this awareness will not change tomorrow
desert or seashore

we've both been here before
I've felt my infatuation for a woman turn to love
and your divorce still seems fresh in your memory
what are we to do with all this emotion
should we let ourselves go
should we not take our love to the next level

we decide that our ceremony should take place here
among the peaks, meadows and streams
only the forest creatures and the universe
will witness the coming together of two souls

our vows will speak of true love
a love that will shine beyond the sun and stars
we know we do not need a paper or pastor to make this truth
perhaps this is our little disguise
we both understand there will be future days when emotions can take over
when the world of work, money, attractive people can run havoc on lovers

but today, right now I pledge myself to you
you mean everything to me that is necessary
your vow also evokes this sentiment
and we seal this all with the best kiss ever
the movie studios could not have staged such a kiss or setting

and now my love
our honeymoon

HOMECOMING

haven't I dreamt
my arrival in our home
coming through the door
hugs and laughter
from the front room to the kitchen

it's been so long, and too long
not to share in your warmth
your love has never stopped pulling me back

I can feel everything
it rests comfortably, here in my heart

keep the light on
I'm only hours away
I am ready to gather all of you in my arms

nurture me again my family

the evening stars guide my path to your door
I am only moments till my past and present are connected

MYSTERY

drifting too far

      years dissolve like clouds in a windy sky

the hunt for freedom

      decisive or deceiving

a strong, moody current carries me along

searching for truth

      adventure

            home

                  balance

                        secrets

SOARING

the medicine woman lightly taps her drum
I lay on my back on a soft blanket
as I close my eyes
I instantly move to a higher, safer place

from eyes of a hawk that soars through the sky a few hundred meters above
I gaze down and I see myself at six years old
I am riding my bicycle at the school grounds
in the same way
I'm also looking up at the hawk from my bike
and I'm also a third party, conceiving both images

as a young boy I'm smiling
these school grounds are familiar
many of my childhood experiences began on these sacred fields
this is where my friends and I gathered to learn how life unfolds
this is where my first fist fight began
we were only innocent kids, not meaning to harm each other
but edged on by the older boys, we tussled
this is where I was surprised by my first kiss from a little girl with long blond hair

the hawk is looking down on all my adventures from my childhood
time seems to stand still
the past and present are moving within each other

looking toward the sky
I see the soft shades of the hawk are white, tan and brown
wings spread
the hawk proudly and gracefully glides throughout the sky
changing altitudes with confidence
this sight lifts my heart like a revelation

soon I am flying next to this magnificent sky creature
soaring to the open horizon and sailing with the wind

I am set free
I am the eyes of the hawk
the eyes of a six year old
and the eyes of the third person that watches with reverence

all three feel that this is a gift
as I ride my bicycle
and as I look down on the ground's activities
as I visualize it all
I grasp the connection

space and infinity are suspended when all three spirits climb together toward heaven

I let the hawk into my life by gently touching my chest three times

the drumming stops
as I sit up
the great bird opens its large wings
and gracefully landing
it slowly settles on my upper back
closing its beautiful wings
the hawk's talons sink into the deep muscles of my back

I feel warmth and peace
trust and wisdom
we are now sacred friends
both hearts beat in time
with the universe and with one spirit

RETURN TO THE DESERT

sky stretching to a lover's lament
grasping my body and soul
this vast color of life's rhythm gathers on a stage of sand

my arms open to the universe,
the air is so dry and clean, that I am swept away with one deep breath
my spirit set free

here in the desert, it's a mystic connection
I feel strong here
perhaps my birth, centuries ago
one of a desert tribe

a child, an elder
someone to look after
someone to look up to

we studied the stars
lived by the changing direction of the sun
huddled together for warmth
drifted apart for insight

my every return here, fills a longing, a prophesy
the desert provides a clear look within my life
my soul, open to the infinite

CELEBRATION OF ART

all of Italy is an art gallery
land of drama, poetry, painting and sculpture
land of beauty
and of women

moved by this country
I see that history saturates life
the hills are healthy with olives, grapes and figs
towns have flavor, full with earthy experience
flesh and blood and vitality
cities stir with excitement
they have a mysterious allure
and the people
these sweet Italians have a gracious, friendly attitude

I was warned that I would fall in love with Italy and all it has to offer
friends advised me about the women
the women will take your breath away
you will marvel and be charmed

although lectured on the magnetic power and pull of the women
I became curious and fascinated
I stepped beyond my understanding
I explored this magic world of grace, style, and grandeur
I became swept up in their skin and curves
their sighs, lips and hips

you're a lavish lover
a sorceress of sensuality
a tender maestra of historic passion and pleasure
you entice and allow me to be part of your celebration
delicate and majestic
you are an esteem prize of age
and a bounty of lustful youth
you're a stunning work of art

Italy, you are not mine to keep
no one owns you
I will gather your rich kisses and smooth skin
your affection and move on
but I will return
it will be difficult to live without you

TIGRESS

lady

you have a dangerous and determined passion

like a tigress giving into temptation

    you stalk and circle your prey

        ravenous, you move in and seize your reward

this tigress will have her desire in her mouth

she won't stop until she and her delighted victim

    are lost in a dreamy state

lover

thank you for this beautiful bliss

FULL MOON MEMORY

tonight I stare up at a bright full moon
the heavenly body stares down upon me
every ocean accepts a lunar tidal change
every lover's memory moves to another full moon
I remember an island, many years ago

we came here often
we shared a small beach cottage
we would walk, hand in hand,
       across long stretches of pure white sand
we played in the clear waters
and marveled at a pirate's treasure of seashells
we collected these jewels
we would surprise each other with these gifts
acting like they were diamonds and rubies
at night, we made love on the beach
covering ourselves with a blanket of the moon's divine light

what a good time we had on that island
a sweet romantic time
we were together
far away from our world back home

that world eventually consumed our island
you and I
our being together

tonight's bright moon covers us both
but in separate locations
we no longer walk the beaches
we no longer find treasures
we no longer sleep together
we are with other lovers

this full moon, with its powerful lunar pull
reminds me of you
I hope you are well tonight

SHIPWRECKED

relentless rain
relentless
so damn much of heaven exploding

beautiful female jaguar
hunting and clawing your way into my soul
is that how you love me
like the relentless rain

imagine my world without you
all those years of caring and sharing
the habit of you

the vessel of our lives together
thrown around on an ocean of love
surviving through storms of passion
torn apart by a world of unfulfilled dreams
torn apart by attractive treasure hunters
plundering our shared secrets
our history
our cherished riches

shipwrecked souls
drifting for years
clinging to any lover
searching for a body to grasp
searching for an equal spirit

the horizon of a new land of love
stepping upon the shore of hope
daring to find true romance
we are blinded by the brilliant glare of fascination
we survive almost drowning
rescued by our inner strength
rescued by a new lover

today we will bury our treasure deep in our hearts
bury our cherished prizes of affection deep in our hearts
deep where only we can find them
where we can always go when we are in need
shipwrecked no more
time has healed the troubled heart
a new ship sails the sea

HOTEL

this lodge sits on a lush hillside about a half a mile to the beach
the open air dining room where we are seated has an adventurous mood
we are the only Americans that are in this group
the one exception is an old expatriate who has fished these waters for decades
he relaxes at a corner table, sipping a cold beer

an international crowd fills the tables with laughter and exotic languages
it was the German couple we had met a few days ago
that told us about this tropical hotel owned by Italians from Milan
we share the room with French, French Canadians, Italians, Danes
three amazing looking women from Chile, and another beauty from Sweden

this is what I like about this land of coconut trees and palms
people from all over the globe
all here to get out of a the cool, cold winter of their homeland
here for the warmth and adventure

expressive words from distant lands are overheard
there is an international seasoning that sits in the air
customs and rituals that I am not familiar with are performed
everyone has their own lifestyle, and it is respected here
we all are sharing in food, music and laughter

the son of the hotel's owner is just getting into surfing
this morning we loaded our boards in his truck
and set out for a secret spot he has been enjoying
we appreciate that he is happy to share his private surf break

we four-wheel through a few small streams
we are told that in the rainy season there is no way to get through those streams
they become deep rivers
we pass through some barbed wired gates
we end on a sandy beach with some fun looking peaks ready to be ridden
which we do, giggling about the privacy and quality of waves

that evening, the Italian cook, a family friend from Milan
is preparing a magnificent meal
apparently, every night, one's appetite is easily satisfied
a full festival of food parades onto the tables for hours

satisfied, I'm finishing my second amaretto over ice
and I'm flirting with one of the ladies from Chile
this is the loveliest siren I have met in a long time
the musical instruments are taken out
soon we are all playing and singing along
as the sultry night unfolds, the live music is replaced with the hotel's favorite CD
and soon a fiery Latin jazz band is belting out some infectious dance music
just what the crowd hungered for and the place goes wild!

I'm dancing with the siren from Chile
this woman knows how to move
most of the entire group from dinner is on the dance floor
arms and bodies jumping to the wild rhythm of the music
the pulse of the conga drums taking us to our limits

the evening finally winds down, it looks like this Chilean beauty and I are a couple
new friends say goodnight
let's all meet at the beach tomorrow

this hotel, the good people, the new friends
and the freedom are why I explore
this is why I journey
I am not looking for anything more than the experience of life
no Shangri-La
no Great Beyond
no hidden paradise
no answer
I found the answer long ago
and I'm thankful

POOL MEDICINE

I have often thought that psychiatrists could cure millions
with a good pool
and the higher states of meditation may
well be achieved by just swimming a mile

50 meter utopia
vacation from the world
taking care of only me
water gypsy fanatic
water as a cure
a remedy

swimming
flowing simplicity
from tip to toe
skin swept clean
muscles stretch
lungs expand
hypnotic breath

moving through water
with water
beyond water

clear
purifying
water

COSTUMES

a veil of mistrust is in that smile
your embrace has no feeling
a well-defined distance is what we have become

at first we felt hurt and wounded
sadness surrounded us both
the fascination and fanfare of new love is long gone

with time, we have moved beyond the bruised emotions
the feeling of emptiness and the moist eyes are not as frequent
we have accepted our going in different directions

and with time, we both feel a certain sense of new independence
we have discovered that our powerful lovemaking isn't for love anymore
there is no fondness or attachment
it is out of instinct, just wanton lust
we are free of any obligation
sadly, I think I enjoy this gritty drive better

I will someday plunge head first into mad love with new woman
hardened by lost love
I will try not to expose those strong emotions
the ones that open the deep area of my heart

this is easy to say, but difficult to believe
and there will be no attempt to stop the discovery
I know the unforeseen splendor of new love
and how we rally in the dream
as if we ascend toward the throne of paradise

the reflective light of a woman
tempted and welcomed
there will be a serenity that only works with a few in life
she and I will discover new worlds about each other

I, of course, will fall
and why not
are we not here to love and live
are we not meant to feel the overwhelming thrill of being charmed
seduced
spellbound
the bewitching of a new fantasy

let fantasy have its fling

CHRISTMAS LOVE

you are calling me from the living room to hurry up
I'm thrilled about the gift you have been hiding from me
with great anticipation, I act like a young boy on Christmas morning
I quickly run into the living room to see what Santa has left me

an enticing voluptuous gift is standing by the tree with a big smile on her face
she is naked except for a small red ribbon that holds her hair up
you make me grin
I'm always amazed how beautiful you are and how sexy you love to act

you lay a thick sheep skin rug down next to the tree
whispering Merry Christmas, you pull me to you
you know how to celebrate the holiday and make this memorable!

later, wrapped in each others arms, we are laughing about the morning
time to hand out presents that have patiently sat under the tree this last week

you hand me a pile of gifts and a card
the note you express is heart felt
and it's just like you to enclose a sexy photo of yourself
you know I'll look at the photo countless times when alone and yearn for you

I give you a gift certificate to your favorite lingerie store
a necklace I found on the other side of the world
and a small expensive bottle of your favorite perfume
it has a soft scent of gardenia that seems to drive me wild!

I thank you for all the thoughtful gifts you graciously gave me
but admit that the greatest gift is simply you being in my life
that small tear in your eye makes this a sensitive moment
you tell me how you love and care for me more than I can imagine

splashing on a touch of your new perfume
we kiss and hug as if we are one
you ask if breakfast can wait....

EXPLOSION IN HEAVEN!

to be in your body

moving

sliding

through the gates of heaven

within the garden of a Goddess

I crave for this gift!

sweetheart

you look fabulous, and on fire!

you are squirming in delight

you are about to explode

lover, violently erupt all over me

I want to feel it fully

I love it!

A GOOD TAN

I've found a small village on the coast of Costa Rica to settle for the winter. I've been without a car, phone and wristwatch for a month now, and don't miss them at all.

There are no utility companies that service this peninsula, so residents are on solar power here. This is a new experience for me, and I've wanted to go native for a while, so it's a welcome adjustment.

My inexpensive rental is in good proximity to a couple of surf spots. It is not the best time of year for strong swells to hit this coast, but I have been riding fun waves every day, and often alone. Lots of water time. I don't think I have been this tan in years.

This is the dry season, so it's easy to cruise here with warm, comfortable daytime temps and not much humidity. I'm feeling free and more robust than I have in a long, long time.

With no one else in the water, I'm learning more about myself. Funny, it seems like the learning never stops!

From the waves, I occasionally spot a youngster who'll be throwing his fishing line into the shallows along the shore. From a distance, the boy walks into my perspective, and as he walks past, he moves away from my perspective, and into the distance.

When out surfing, the water is alive with activity. I keep alert to any danger, but I figure there are plenty of plump fish out here for the larger creatures in the food chain to eat besides me.

After a morning of surfing and breakfast, I'm back at the beach. I've been wandering the shoreline for shells and ideas for the book. I've been writing quite a lot of verse while staying here. Potentially, good compositions are saved, and of course, some get thrown away. One obscure discarded line may show up later in another piece.

At night by candlelight, I've been pouring out the words on paper. Lots of editing and rewrites, but there is a welcome feeling of fulfillment when you know your poem or your short story is complete. And, I work on few scripted projects at the same time. This way I can return to a concept and find new inspiration.

Sometimes, writing is a gentle struggle, and sometimes, it's intuitive and appropriate words come with clarity. I enjoy the whole process.

My colorful shells fill little nooks and crannies at the cottage where I live. My surfboard sits in an alcove near the door. There are cozy chairs to lounge in, the bed is comfortable, and there's a nice porch out front for early morning tea. The place is soulful.

The cottage has screens instead of windows lining the upper-third of the walls. This allows the afternoon sea breeze to flow unmolested throughout the house. A pleasing mango tree and some moody palms rest satisfied in the front yard. The house fits my needs quite well for the next few months.

I often watch the sunset from a local restaurant. There's a panoramic view, and the sweet sound of the surf resonates below. Besides making a great margarita, the fresh fish is grilled to perfection!

Life moves slowly here on this sunlit coast. It's difficult to think about donning a wetsuit again and surfing the cold water back home in California. I'm getting a lot of writing done, the waves are building in size, and there are new shells to discover. Maybe I'll just stay here for the next few months and work on my tan.

www.ingramcontent.com/pod-product-compliance
Lightning Source LLC
Chambersburg PA
CBHW080843250626
47163CB00003B/430